He is good at studying,
good at painting,
and good at singing.

3

I am his little sister Marie,
who is good at nothing!

4

We Are Proud of You

Written by Ye-shil Kim
Illustrated by The Pope Twins
Edited by Joy Cowley

My big brother
is good at everything.

He always does well in school.

I am not good at studying,
not good at painting,
and not good at singing.

I am so stupid!
I feel really bad.

Then a voice says,
"No, you're not stupid!"

Who is talking?

Oh! It is my stuffed rabbit.
I say to him, "Really?
Can you tell me one thing
that I am good at?"

"Hi everybody," says my rabbit.
"Do you know Marie?
What kind of kid is she?"

"Of course, I do!"

Marie's neighbours

Rabbit says,

"You are Marie's aunt, right?
Tell me about Marie."

Marie's loving aunt

"Marie is a good cook," says Aunt.
"Her salads are delicious
and so are her pancakes.
I think she's a better cook than me!"

Rabbit goes to Marie's parents.
"Say something about your Marie."

12

"My Marie is such a fast runner," says Mum.

"Yes!" says Dad. "She runs so fast, you can't see her feet."

Marie's Mum and Dad

13

Rabbit asks Marie's ballet teacher,
"Does Marie dance well?"

"Of course she does!" says the teacher.
"She is like a fluttering butterfly."

Marie is her ballet teacher's best student.

15

"Tell me about Marie!"
Rabbit says to Marie's grandmother.

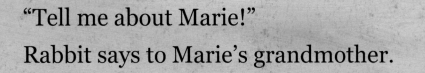

Grandmother is as busy as Marie.

"She is always busy," says Grandmother.
"She runs errands and cleans her room."

"Teacher," says Rabbit,
"what kind of student is Marie?"

Teacher loves to have Marie in her class.

18

"She is a very happy girl,"
says the teacher.
"She is always full of fun."

"Hey, kids!" says Rabbit.
"What kind of friend is Marie?"

Marie's classmates are her friends too.

The friends all talk at once.

"She is really funny."

"She is very popular."

"Marie is the best!"

"All right, Big Brother!" says Rabbit.
"Say something about your sister Marie."

22

Big Brother smiles. "I want to say that I'm very proud that I'm her big brother."

The most wonderful brother in the world.

Marie said to Rabbit,
"Me? Am I really like that?"

24

Everyone cried,
"Of course you are!
We are all proud of you!"

25

My dear lovely bright little girl,

You always think that I love your brother more.
And you always seem to have so little confidence in yourself,
comparing yourself with your brother.
I'm really sad whenever I hear you doing that.
Don't you know how special you are?
There are lots of things you are good at!
I've never seen a girl like you who greets everyone you meet,
is friendly to everyone, and is so hardworking and funny.
Never compare yourself with your brother or anybody else.
You are the only one of you. There is no one like you
in the whole wide world. I love you and love you, my little girl!

With love, Your mum

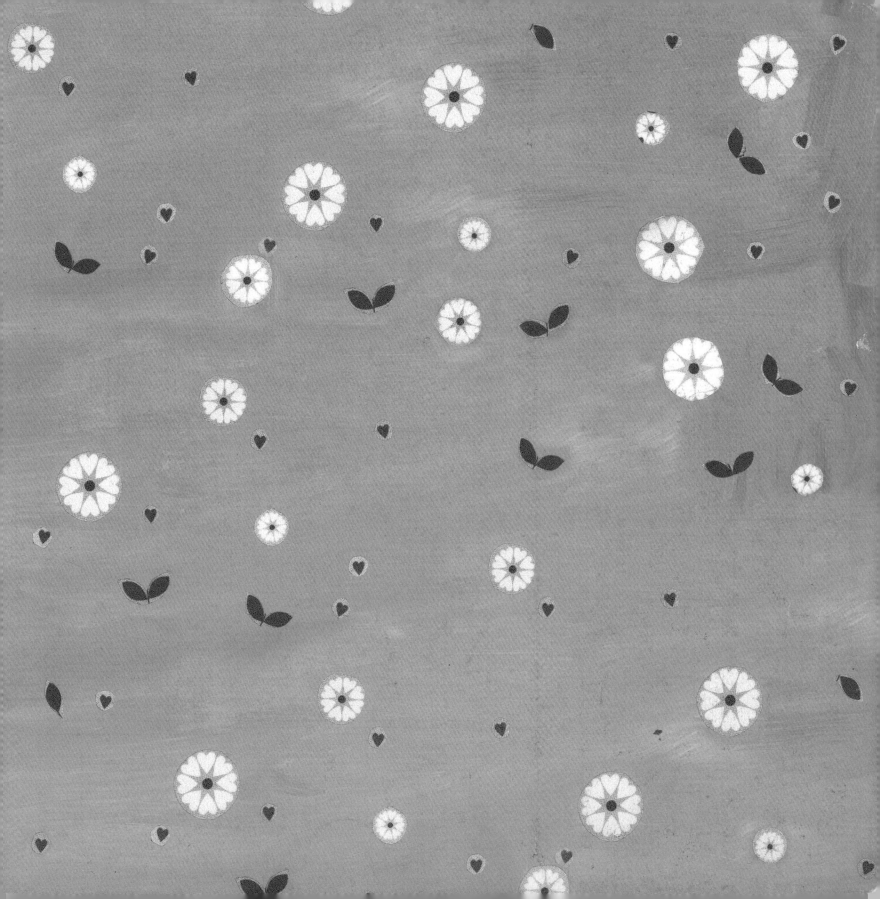

big & SMALL

Original Korean text by Ye-shil Kim
Illustrations by The Pope Twins
Original Korean edition © Eenbook

This English edition published by big & SMALL
by arrangement with Eenbook
English text edited by Joy Cowley
Additional editing by Mary Lindeen
Artwork for this edition produced
in cooperation with Norwood House Press, U.S.A.
English edition © big & SMALL 2015

ISBN: 978-1-925233-87-2

Printed in Korea